A GEEKS AND THINGS COZY MYSTERY

Saints and Sinners

S.E. BIGLOW

 Created with Vellum

1

The sun shone hot overhead as Kalina picked her way through the gravestones in the cemetery beside the church. Halfway to her destination she stopped and pressed a hand to her side, letting the muscle cramp work itself out. Her other hand supported her swollen belly. Pregnancy and summer heat were not a good combination but it would soon be over. With her due date fast approaching, she wouldn't have to worry about the swollen ankles much longer. Gaining her second wind, she trudged forward over damp grass—recently doused by the sprinklers—finally stopping at the grave in question: her father's. He'd been gone over a year but it still felt like she was saying her last goodbye at the funeral. Tears welled in her eyes and she let them fall. So much had happened in that year. She'd found her way back home to Ellesworth, MA and her family's comic book shop. It sated her need to be nerdy and gave her a purpose. And she'd found love again with her first love: Christian Harper. They'd been through betrayals and loss together but he'd also risen from detective to captain. And now they were married and about to become parents.

A few weeds poked up around the base of her father's headstone and she did her best to pluck them without being able to bend over properly. "Hi, Dad." She wiped at her cheeks with her free hand. "I know it's been a while since I visited and I'm sorry for that. I've just had a lot going on. Chris and I got married in January. You would have loved it. And you're about to be a grandfather again. It's a girl.

"I've kept the shop running just as you had it. Well, with a few technology upgrades. We're doing great business and it's reminded me how much I missed being there. It feels like home and when I'm there, I'm a little closer to you."

Fresh tears stained her cheeks and a breath caught in her throat. She hadn't expected this visit to be quite as emotional. But she was moving forward in her life without him and it hit her that there were so many things she'd longed to ask him that she'd never get answered. Sure, she had her mother and sister for support but sometimes a girl just needed her father.

Beads of sweat trickled down her neck in the summer warmth but she stayed where she was, hands resting at her sides, one still gripping the scraggly weeds. The silence of the cemetery pressed in around her and what should have been a comfort carried a sense of foreboding. The moisture on her next turned chilly in the summer air and butterflies danced in her stomach. Something had disturbed her peaceful, if teary, visit.

Casting the weeds aside, she made her way deeper into the cemetery. Simple headstone and ground-level plaques gave way to taller monuments to those who had passed on. Some had seen their fair share of rough weather. Engravings had worn down and were only partially legible. Some had seen their edges eroded over time. She stopped to study some of them, curious to see who lay beneath them. She recognized a few names from town history. There was an entire row of Finnegan family members, which only served to turn her stomach. Shortly before the wedding, Kalina and Chris had solved a series of deaths linked to a career-ladder climbing journalist and her love-struck cousin. Beth had been the latest generation of Finnegans in town. Kalina hurried past the rows and stopped when she spotted something sticking out between a couple of the tallest headstones. Shadows cast by the trees overhead obscured the area, forcing her to get closer to investigate.

She rubbed her belly as the baby kicked a time or two, landing solid shots to her ribs. The movement winded her temporarily and she had to stop and catch her breath again. "Thanks for that, baby girl." She massaged the left side of her ribs until the pain lessened and she could continue forward.

The object that had caught her eye was a designer pump, dark brown and sharply pointed at the toe. Said shoe was still attached to a woman's slender foot. Kalina moved between the two headstones to find a young woman, a few years younger than herself, laying between the graves with an angry red pool of blood congealing on her chest. Her eyes were still open, frozen in a look of what

Kalina could only describe as curiosity. Whoever this woman had been, the fatal blow had
not come as a shock. Beyond her designer
footwear, she was dressed in an impeccable
knee-length summer dress. It clung to her
curves even as she lay sprawled on the ground
in death. Her hair was still pinned up on the
side of her head. Only a tiny trickle of blood
marred her pale pink lips.

The shock of the discovery finally hit
Kalina a minute later and she backpedaled as
fast as possible. This wasn't the first dead
body of unknown but definitely suspicious
causes she'd seen in the last year. In fact, she'd
seen more than she'd ever cared to in her
thirty-four years of life. But that bug that bit
her every time something like this happened
in town took hold of her thoughts as she
searched for her phone. This was going to be
her last case. After the baby was born, she
wouldn't have the time to go running off digging up clues. Her priorities needed to change

and she'd accepted that. But this one intrigued her and she knew herself well enough to admit that she wasn't going to let this beautiful woman go. She finally found her phone and hit the first number on the speed dial: her husband.

"Hey honey. Is everything OK with the baby?"

"The baby's fine. But you need to get down to the cemetery and bring a coroner. I just found a body."

2

$\mathcal{K}$alina kept a tight grip on her phone while she waited for Chris to arrive. The sun continued to beat down, making the scene even more unpleasant. She studied the woman's face in an effort to avoid looking at the bloody wound in her chest. Something about her eyes and the way her hair swooped down from her hairline made her look familiar. Sure, being the proprietor of the only shop that sold all things nerdy meant she came into contact with a large portion of the town, but that didn't mean she knew everyone. Still, something about this woman tickled a faint memory at the very edges of Kalina's memory.

She longed to check the woman for ID to sate her curiosity but she was a cop's wife and she knew better. Instead, she walked the perimeter around the gravestones, noting shoe depressions in the damp grass. Whoever had done this had been here recently, which likely meant she hadn't died long ago. It was bold, killing someone in broad daylight, even in a cemetery. As she rounded the second headstone, she noted a few flecks of red marring the pale granite stonework. She'd been killed here. Rubbing her lower back as she came to stand back where she'd started, she took note of whose graves bookended the dead woman's body.

Abigail and Harrison Fischer.

The names, much like the woman's face, rang a distant bell in her memory but it was so far buried she couldn't grab hold of it and bring it forward. A breeze picked up and tugged at the hem of her shirt and the stray hairs hanging out of the messy bun on top of her head.

"Kal!"

She turned toward the sound of her name and a broad grin broke out on her face. Chris trudged toward her, a few uniformed officers lagged behind him. She stayed put and waited for him. How had he known where to find her?

"How'd you find me?"

"GPS on your phone."

"You are tracking me now?"

"Only so I know where you are in case something happens with the baby."

She laughed. "You do realize that's kind of stalker behavior, right?"

"I was kidding. I called Clinton Mason to check the surveillance video to find where you were."

"There's surveillance cameras in the cemetery? Isn't that a little creepy? Watching people mourn their loved ones. It's supposed to be private."

"We had some vandalism a few months back," a deep bass voice said.

Clinton Mason was a thick-necked man with shaggy hair sticking up at odd angles along his head. He apparently didn't own a comb or, if he did, didn't know how to use it. His torso and upper body were beefy and muscled under his short-sleeved shirt.

"Who would vandalize a cemetery?' she asked.

"Kids on dares mostly."

"I didn't see any signs warning about a security system when I came in."

"You wouldn't. We don't advertise them. It gives those coming here to spend time with their loved ones the privacy they deserve," Clinton said.

"So you caught whoever did this on cameras. That should make it an easy investigation."

"Well, we hope we did. See"—Clinton pointed to the trees overhanging the Fischer graves—"the angle is a bit sharp on these so we may not get a clear picture."

"But we'll know for sure when it happened," Chris said.

The uniformed officers finally caught up with the small group already gathered and Kalina realized one was carrying an evidence collection kit. She shifted her weight as the baby moved and the slight change in her stance caught Chris's attention.

"Clint, can we go see that video footage? I think my wife wouldn't mind sitting down in the air conditioning for a while."

"Oh, yeah. Sure thing, Captain."

Kalina took Chris's hand and they followed Clinton back to the single story building used for wakes. She hadn't been there since her father's service but it was exactly as she remembered. For a funeral parlor it was brightly lit and decorated. It gave off an almost cheery feel. The air conditioning was on high blast when they walked in and it sent shivers down her back and turned the sweat slicking her skin cold.

"The video monitors are right through here," Clint said and led them into a room she hadn't noticed before.

A computer with a single monitor sat on a squat mahogany desk. The screen flared to life when Clint jiggled the mouse, displaying four quadrants, each with a different angle. Without doing anything, the angles changed to display another four locations throughout the cemetery. Clint settled in front of the machine and after a few keystrokes brought up a single angle. Kalina saw the officers and the forensic technician bent over the body.

"Roll it back a couple hours," Chris said.

"You got it." Clint hit a button and the video began to rewind. Kalina watched as the last few minutes passed by in reverse. She tried not to feel embarrassed when Chris caught her circling the gravestones.

"I was just trying to see if there was anything else there," she said, feeling the need to explain herself.

"I didn't say anything," Chris said and placed a hand on her shoulder.

The image on the screen continued to pass by in reverse. Kalina disappeared entirely but the body remained. No one approached or moved away for forty minutes according to the time stamp and then, finally, a hooded figure appeared, walking backwards until he bent over the woman's body.

"Can you get a better look at his face?" Chris asked.

"Not from this angle."

The man stepped back and they could just make out a knife being pulled from her chest.

"At least it looks like we nailed down time

of death for you," Clint said and pointed a meaty finger at the timestamp.

10:47 a.m.

They watched as the man backed up and the woman stood up, now alive. They appeared to be talking and then they disappeared off screen entirely.

"I'll see what I can do to clean up the footage. See what other angles I can find that they might have passed," Clint said.

"Good, thanks." Chris tugged on Kalina's arm. "I'm taking you back to the station. You need to give a statement."

3

Kalina didn't want to leave the cool air of the office but she allowed Chris to lead her back outside into the heat and toward the parking lot abutting the church. She fanned herself as he unlocked the squad car he'd come over in. Her car sat a few spaces away.

"Can't we take mine? I'll probably just head over to the shop for a little while when I'm finished at the station."

"OK." He hit the button to lock the squad

car again and followed her a few spaces over. "You want me to drive?"

She flashed him a smile. "I'm perfectly capable of driving, thank you. Besides, I've got the seat where I want it and I don't want you messing with it."

He held his hands up in surrender and rounded the front of the car to the passenger side. She settled in behind the wheel and started the engine. Chris buckled up beside her and studied something out the passenger side window. Kalina followed his gaze and spotted the uniformed officers loading the woman's body onto a stretcher.

Chris looked back at her. "How'd you find her?"

Kalina pulled out of the parking lot and headed toward the station. "It's hard to explain. I was visiting my dad's grave and then I just got this feeling like something was just ... off. I wandered a little and then I found her. I guess it was luck or something."

"Or a mother's intuition to protect her child," he said and she caught a small smile out of the corner of her eye.

"Maybe, but regardless of what it was, I'm glad she was found so quickly. It has to give you and your officers a better chance of finding the man who did this."

"Here's hoping Clint can get a better angle on the man's face."

She eased to a stop at a crosswalk, allowing a gaggle of teenage girls to scurry past. "Speaking of faces, hers looked familiar somehow."

"What do you mean?"

"Well, it was mostly her eyes that made me look twice. I swear I've seen her somewhere before, maybe a long time ago. It's like there's a memory buried in my brain but I just can't reach it."

Before Chris could answer, his phone buzzed and he answered the call. "Captain Harper." A pause and he pinched the bridge of his nose. "OK. Well, take prints and we'll run them and see what comes up."

"What was that about?" she asked and made the final turn leading up to the police station parking lot.

"She didn't have any photo ID on her so they're going to run her prints and maybe we'll get lucky."

She pulled into a spot near the front door and killed the engine. Chris was out of the car and opening the driver side door before she'd had a chance to unbuckle her seatbelt and yank the keys from the ignition. She squeezed his hand as he helped her out of the car.

"Are you really doing OK with all of this?" he asked as they walked side by side into the station.

"Yes. She isn't the first dead body I've seen, Chris." *Even if it is the last.* She'd tell him about that promise she'd made to herself when this was over.

"I'm not trying to be overbearing. I just want you and the baby to be safe."

She leaned into his shoulder. "I know. And I appreciate that. More than you know."

"I also know you aren't going to let this drop. So just run whatever you find by me or Jimmy."

"Got it. And don't take any risks," she added.

"Exactly."

He held the door open for her and Jimmy greeted them before they'd made it past the reception desk. When all of her adventures in crime solving had begun a year ago, Jimmy had been a fresh-faced, newly minted officer. He'd grown a lot since then. She was pretty sure he'd actually added a few inches in height as well as the full beard he now sported. It made him look much older than his early twenties. He'd also grown as an offi-cer. Only a few months ago he'd saved her from a knife wielding madman.

"They radioed from the scene. I'll take her statement," he said.

Kalina caught the look of pride on Chris's face as he headed for his office, leaving her and Jimmy alone. Silence fell between them for a moment and then Jimmy's business-like exterior melded a little.

"Come on, let's get you off your feet."

"You know, he may not say it but he's really proud of you," she said in a hushed tone.

"I try. I'm just glad he's been around. I have something to strive for, you know?"

"Well, he notices it. Keep it up and you'll make detective before you know it."

Jimmy gave a nervous laugh and led her over to a vacant desk in the bull pen. The computer was already displaying a blank witness statement form, ready for her words to fill it. Without having to ask, he put in her contact information and then turned to face her. "So, tell me everything you can remember."

Kalina was about to fill him in on her graveyard visit when the forensic technician from the cemetery burst through the front doors and barreled past them to Chris's office. He didn't even bother knocking. She couldn't hear what was being said but she didn't have to wait long to find out what had the man so agitated.

"What's wrong, boss?" Jimmy asked as Chris approached them.

"The fingerprints came back. They belong to a Verona Maxwell."

"Why is he so upset then?" Kalina pointed toward the technician.

"Because they also belong to a dead girl."

4

Both Kalina and Jimmy stared in silence at Chris, letting the revelation sink in. It wasn't possible for two people to have the same fingerprints. Not even identical twins had the same prints. Kalina opened her mouth to ask the obvious question but Jimmy beat her to it.

"Who was the girl?"

"Paige Fischer."

"Wait, I know that name," Kalina said and

looked between the two men. "She was a couple years younger than me. She died in an accident or something when she was ten or eleven if I remember right."

Chris nodded. "She and her brother, Patrick, both drowned."

"But how does the department even have their prints? Did they take them when they found the bodies?" Kalina asked.

Chris shook his head and held up a pair of files with pictures of a young boy and girl. "Their parents had them printed in case something ever happened. Or so the files say."

"What, did they expect someone to kidnap them?" Jimmy scoffed.

"They might have," Kalina answered. "They were one of the richest families in town. I just remember other kids whispering about them when they started at public school."

"You've got a better memory of them than I do."

"You wouldn't have interacted with them much. My mom insisted I do a youth mentorship program the school year before they died. It was to help younger kids improve their literacy."

"No offense but if they were rich kids, couldn't their parents have afforded tutors or something?" Jimmy said.

Kalina's face fell at the thought of the pair of them. So young and inseparable. "Looking back, I don't think their parents really wanted to spend much time with them."

"Can't we just ask them if their daughter could still be alive?"

"No. Verona, if that's her real name, was found between the Fischers' graves. I didn't notice when they'd died but they're definitely both gone."

Chris set the files on the desk in front of Jimmy and massaged his temple. "I'm going to have the lab run the prints again."

"What about a DNA test?" Kalina suggested.

"If we can find something that belonged to Paige Fischer when she was ten then maybe."

Something about the girl's death was gnawing at Kalina's memory. She needed to get to the shop to do some digging. "I'm going to finish giving Jimmy my statement and then head to the shop to check on Jill and AJ."

"Good. I'm going to see what I can find about the deaths of Paige and Patrick Fischer," Chris said and disappeared back to his office.

"This is going to be a weird one, isn't it, Kal?" Jimmy said as soon as Chris was out of earshot.

"Yeah, I think it is."

Twenty minutes later, she'd signed the statement and was back behind the wheel of her car. It was a short trip back to Main Street and the family-owned comic shop she'd inherited from her father. As she pulled up to the turn off for the lot behind the building, a sense of satisfaction warmed her. There was a steady stream of people coming and going. Business was booming. She made her way inside through the back door, which led into the game room. A group of teenagers sat huddled around one of the tables, snickering into whatever they'd drawn in Cards against Humanity. They didn't react as she walked by and out to the front of the shop. Her sister, Jillian, stood behind the counter taking a five dollar bill from a boy who couldn't have been older than seven or eight. Kalina watched as his eyes widened when Jillian handed over the package of comics safely sealed in protective covers.

"Hey," Kalina said once the kid and his mother were gone.

Jillian jumped. "Kal, you scared me. What are you doing here?"

"I wanted to make sure everything was going OK."

"Everything is fine. Although those kids

back there have been very quiet."

"Don't worry about them. I actually needed to ask you something."

Jillian pulled the stool over and Kalina settled atop it. "What's on your mind, little sister?"

"Do you remember Paige and Patrick Fischer? They died in a drowning accident about fifteen years ago."

Her sister rubbed at her chin in thought. "Sort of. I think Mom took us to a memorial service or a candlelight vigil."

"What do you remember about what happened to them?"

"Just what the papers said. They were out at the beach and one of them got swept up in a wave and the other one went out to save them."

"But they never found their bodies."

"I don't know, Kal. Why?"

"I was visiting Dad's grave today and I found a dead woman."

"It was a cemetery."

"Not one who'd been buried. Chris ran her fingerprints and they matched Paige Fischer's."

"But that isn't possible."

"It wouldn't be if she was actually dead. But what if she survived and someone found out?"

"Who would care all these years later?"

"I don't know. But she was left between her parents' graves. If this woman really is Paige, someone out there knew the truth and killed her for it."

Jillian let out a groan. "You're getting dragged into this. Don't get dragged into this. Not now."

"I can't help it. And this is the last one, I swear. After this I'm out."

""You better be. Or else we'll be going to your funeral because Chris will have killed you himself."

Kalina laughed. "Thanks for the support.

Why don't you go grab some lunch? I can man the counter for a little while. Besides, I miss being here. Sitting at home was getting really boring."

"Only you could think getting ready for a baby was boring."

Before Kalina could get out a retort, Jillian headed out into the sunshine. Kalina retrieved her tablet from below the counter and pulled up the town's newspaper archives. Because she couldn't remember the exact date of the drowning, she input "Fischer twins death" into the search bar at the top of the page and waited for it to populate results.

The first result was their joint obituary from August of 1995. It was a brief paragraph with a photo of the twins side by side with the ocean as a backdrop. The next result, dated July 31, 1995, appeared to be the first article about the circumstances surrounding their mysterious drowning.

Fischer Children Lost At Sea

By: Andrew Fisk, Staff Reporter

It is a sad day for the people of Ellesworth as two of its youngest citizens were lost at sea. Ten-year-old Paige Fischer and her twin brother, Patrick, were presumed dead today after the family's boat, which went missing from the family's slip off the beach three days ago, was found abandoned near the shore near Marblehead, Massachusetts. Authorities say the children were believed to be aboard the ship when it went missing. No bodies have yet been recovered.

Mr. and Mrs. Fischer refused comment as they grieve the loss of their children. Some in town are suspicious of the way the children died. One neighbor, who wished to remain anonymous, noted that the parents didn't report the children missing until they received a call that the boat had been located. Others questioned how the children could have had access to the boat without adult supervision. It is unknown at this time whether the authorities will be investigating Abigail and Harrison Fischer for their role in the deaths.

Kalina's pulse quickened as she reread the second paragraph. The Fischers hadn't even reported their children missing. Her recollection that they hadn't been very involved parents came back to her with full force. Surely they couldn't have had anything to do with it. Even absent parents wouldn't purposely send their children to their deaths. There was one final result on the list. A follow-up article dated August 21, 1995.

Fischers Cleared of Wrongdoing in Tragic Death of Twins

By: Andrew Fisk, Staff Reporter

Less than a month after the family's

boat was found off the shore of Marblehead, MA without the Fischer children aboard, the police have cleared Abigail and Harrison Fischer of any wrongdoing in the deaths of ten-year-old twins Patrick and Paige. A source close to the police shared that the parents were out of town on a business trip during the time the boat went missing.

The children had been in the care of their nanny, Lois Hendrix. According to a statement from Mr. and Mrs. Fischer, Ms. Hendrix has been fired and charges have been filed. A source in the prosecutor's office declined to comment but it is expected Ms. Hendrix will take a plea deal if offered to avoid a trial.

Well, that was interesting. She didn't remember a nanny being around when she spent her summer reading to both children. Then again, she'd been wrapped up in her own life and her own friends as soon as the reading time was over. At least now she had something to follow up on while Chris and Jimmy determined whether Verona Maxwell really was Paige Fischer. Perhaps Lois Hendrix would know what happened to the Fischers too. But first she needed to find the woman. She didn't want to let Chris in on this lead until she had something concrete to tell him so she placed a call to the one person who might know the town's older, sordid secrets, Mrs. Margaret Grant. She'd been one of former Captain Daniel Cahill's targets for lying on the stand at his father's murder trial. She and Kalina had kept in touch since the ordeal.

"Hello?" Margaret's voice was weak thanks to the partial paralysis she'd suffered at Cahill's hands.

"Hi Mrs. Grant, it's Kalina Greystone. How are you doing?"

"Fine. And I told you to call me Margaret."

"Right, sorry. I was hoping I could come by. I have something I need to ask you about."

"Yes, dear. Please do come by."

5

———

After waiting for Jillian to get back to the shop, Kalina headed out to visit Mrs. Grant. She pulled up to the small front porch and found Mrs. Grant waiting outside. Kalina gave a wave as she climbed out of the car and made her way up to sit beside the older woman.

"My, look at you!" Margaret exclaimed.

"Due in a few weeks," Kalina said and rubbed her belly as the baby kicked.

"I take it the little one isn't what you wanted to talk about."

"No. It's not. Do you remember Patrick and Paige Fischer?"

Margaret nodded her head more vigorously than Kalina had seen her do in almost a year. "Such a tragedy. Poor dears, lost so young."

"Do you remember what happened to their nanny, Lois Hendrix? She was charged with their deaths."

"She did some time in prison but only a few years."

"Do you know where she ended up when she got out?"

"Why the sudden interest?"

Kalina blew out a breath. "We found a body who we think might be Paige Fischer. But she wasn't a child. She was an adult. I'm just trying to figure out if it's possible she might have survived the boat accident. I thought Lois could tell me what she knew from when they went missing."

"I heard she ended up settling down in Boston. Getting lost in the big city you know. No one there would know what she'd done."

"Thank you," Kalina said with a smile.

"Don't give it up, dear."

"Sorry?"

'This knack you've got for digging until you get the truth."

"My priorities are changing."

"Maybe but there will come a time when it will be right to pick it back up. Don't let it die completely. Promise me." The woman's tone was firm and her voice was as clear as the first time they'd talked.

"I promise." Kalina gripped the woman's partially paralyzed hand and gave a firm squeeze.

They sat in silence for a short time, both enjoying the sun on their faces. Inevitably the baby moved, landing a solid thump to her bladder and the spell broke. She knew she needed to talk to Lois Hendrix but she had no real reason to seek her out. Showing up on her doorstep unannounced asking about the Fischer children would likely close the woman off to answering questions. But she wasn't ready to share what she'd found with Chris yet.

"I should get going. Thanks again for letting me stop by," she said and bent as best she could to give the woman a hug. "Do you want me to help you back in?"

"Oh, no. I'll be fine here a while."

With a final wave, Kalina headed back to her car. As soon as she'd buckled up, she put her phone on speaker and placed a call to the station.

"Ellesworth PD," Jimmy answered.

"Jimmy, it's Kalina. I need you to do me a favor."

"I'm listening."

"I need you to find the last known address

for Lois Hendrix. I think she lives in Boston. Would have moved there maybe fifteen years ago."

"That name came up in some of the files I was reviewing."

"I know. She was the Fischers' nanny. She went to jail for a while over their deaths."

"And you think I should talk to her."

"I think I should go with you to talk to her."

"I'm not sure the captain would like that."

"I can make her feel at ease. Besides, you'd be surprised what a belly full of baby can get you," she said and patted just above her belly button.

"I'll see what I can find and text you."

"You're the best."

"Bye."

The connection died after Jimmy hung up and she focused on her short drive home. Even if she wasn't ready to tell Chris what she'd found, she did need to let him know where she was going and that it wouldn't be alone. She found him already at home on the couch staring at files. An untouched—and likely cold—cup of coffee sat on the side table next to him.

"Hi honey," she said.

He jumped at the sound of her voice, clearly oblivious to her presence. "Sorry. I thought you'd already be home."

"I stopped by the shop to check on Jill and then I paid Margaret Grant a visit. I hadn't seen her in a while."

"How is she doing?"

"Well, she's not entering anything into the Solstice Fair this year but she is in pretty good spirits."

He looked up from the folder in front of him and patted the vacant spot on the couch. "There's something else. What is it?"

"I may have found someone who can help figure out if Paige survived that boat accident.

I didn't want to get your hopes up so I asked Jimmy to look into it."

"Who'd you find?"

"Lois Hendrix."

"Their nanny."

"That's part of the reason I went to go see Margaret. She told me that after Lois got out of prison, she moved away, to Boston. I want to talk to her. She must remember something. And maybe she knows what happened to Abigail and Harrison."

"It's worth a try. But don't be surprised if she doesn't want to talk to you."

"I know. But we have to try."

She looked at the myriad casefiles spread over the table. "What's all this?"

"I pulled the files on the twins' disappearance and supposed deaths. I also got the results back from the second fingerprint test."

"Let me guess, they still say Verona Maxwell and Paige Fischer are the same person."

"Yes. I'm even more convinced that she's

the same person because before 1996 Verona Maxwell didn't exist. No birth certificate, no social security number. Nothing."

Kalina cocked her head in thought. "And then all of a sudden she's got all those things."

"Yeah. I managed to reach out to her parents. They're from out of town but I'm having them come in tomorrow. Either way, I need to notify them of their daughter's murder."

Kalina sighed and settled back on the couch. "Did Clint ever get you more useable footage of the killer?"

Chris let out a sigh of his own and shook his head. "He sent some more over but the techs are having a hell of a time cleaning it up. Whoever this guy is, he was careful not to let his face get caught on any of the cameras. He must have scoped out the cemetery before he took her there."

"He couldn't have been that smart. He left her somewhere that had a really good angle of her body. If I hadn't found her, someone else would have."

"I'm starting to think he wanted her to be found."

Kalina's phone beeped with a new text message, interrupting the conversation. She glanced at it. Jimmy had been successful in tracking down Lois Hendrix and he would pick her up the following morning at 7.

"That's early," Chris said and gave her a sympathetic smile.

"We need to beat the traffic. Besides, I'm guessing she has a job and us showing up unannounced is going to throw a big wrench in her day." She pushed herself to her feet and headed towards the kitchen. "Come on, let's eat. I'm starving."

"I'll be there in a minute."

She left him in the living room and listened as he made a call. She rummaged in the fridge, gathering ingredients to make chicken salad, suddenly craving a nice, thick sandwich.

"Jimmy, it's Chris. Yes, I know about tomorrow. Call ahead and set up a time. Leave earlier if you have to." A pause. "No I'll make sure she's ready. Thanks."

She said nothing as he joined her by the sink and began pulling big leaves of lettuce off the head and running them under water. She was going to need to go to bed early if there was the possibility of Jimmy coming by earlier than expected.

6

———

The sun was barely above the horizon line as Kalina packed a thermos full of decaf tea and some oatmeal into her bag. Chris stood bleary-eyed by her side at the front door, both waiting for Jimmy to arrive. He'd made arrangements to meet Lois Hendrix at 8:00 at a coffee shop before she went to work. According to him, Lois had been more than willing to talk about the Fischer children.

"Good luck today," Chris said, yawning.

"You, too," she answered and gave him a sideways hug. She hoped today would prove fruitful for both of them, getting the police that much closer to finding the killer.

Jimmy's hybrid pulled into the driveway and, after a quick kiss, Kalina headed out and crammed herself into the front seat. In the end, she had to push it almost all the way back to get comfortable. "So she sounded willing to talk?" she asked once they'd finally hit the highway.

"Yeah. I didn't give her much but she's willing to sit down with us so that's a start."

"I hope Chris can find something from Verona's parents."

Jimmy accelerated and shifted into the high occupancy lane. As the car settled into doing just over 60 MPH, he glanced across at her. "What do you think happened?"

Kalina shrugged. "I don't know. Maybe she survived the accident. She could have had some kind of head trauma that made her forget who she was and someone found her."

"But who would want her dead? I mean killing her at her parents' graves is pretty specific. Whoever it was knew she was really Paige Fischer."

"Until we talk to Lois Hendrix, I can't say with any certainty what could have happened."

The car fell silent as Jimmy focused on navigating the increased traffic on the roads. Kalina took the opportunity to doze, her head propped against the window of the passenger side door. The gentle, steady hum of the engine and the tires on the pavement lulled her into a peaceful unconsciousness until Jimmy slammed on the brakes.

"What happened?" She jolted upright.

"Sorry, the idiot in front of me didn't have his blinker on until the last second. I nearly hit him."

She waited for her heart rate to lower back

to normal and managed to stay awake the rest of the trip. The edge of the city soon came into view and she dug her thermos and oatmeal from her bag, sipping the still warm tea.

"So where are we meeting her exactly?"

"Coffee shop in downtown."

"Good luck finding parking around there."

He quirked a brow at her but said nothing. She tried not to laugh at his frustration as half an hour later he drove down one-way streets looking for a place to park. The clock on the dash ticked away the minutes until their meeting with Lois.

"Just let me out by the coffee shop and I'll start without you," she said.

With a huff, he pulled up to the curb and she climbed out with some difficulty. She wouldn't have minded sticking with him until he found a spot except the baby was happily punting her bladder like a soccer ball and she was in desperate need of a bathroom.

Five minutes later, she scanned the small

crowd in the coffee shop, hoping she would recognize Lois Hendrix. She pulled up her phone and tried to find the one photo she'd seen of the woman at the end of the article about her arrest. It was several decades out of date but it was enough for her to cautiously approach the woman with greying hair sitting by the window, a large coffee grasped between slender fingers.

"Ms. Hendrix?"

The woman looked over. "Yes."

Kalina slid into the chair opposite her. "My name is Kalina Greystone."

"You aren't the officer I spoke with yesterday."

"I'm with him. He's parking."

"Not from around here."

"No, he's definitely not a city boy."

"What's got the police in Ellesworth looking me up after all these years? I did my time but I never hurt those children."

Kalina was torn. She wanted to dive in and

get what she could but she knew Jimmy wouldn't be happy with her.

"Maybe we should wait until Jim—Officer Griggs gets here."

Lois drummed her fingers on the side of her cup. "Please, just tell me what this is about."

"A woman was found yesterday and her fingerprints match Paige Fischer's."

If Lois hadn't already been sitting down Kalina was sure she would have fallen at the news. "She was alive all this time?"

"It seems that way. We were just hoping you might be able to fill in some of the gaps about what really happened the day they went missing."

"I'll never forget that day."

The door to the shop opened and Jimmy stalked in, his neck and cheeks red. He was clearly not happy. Kalina pointed him to the counter and mimed drinking. He would be less irritable with some caffeine in his system.

"Ms. Hendrix, I presume," Jimmy said once he'd acquired an extra-large iced coffee and dragged a chair over to the table.

"Officer Griggs. Ms. Greystone was just telling me you found Paige."

"Yes, ma'am. She was going by the name Verona Maxwell."

"I don't know where the last name came from but she loved Shakespeare."

"She was adopted by a foster family," Jimmy answered.

"She was a little young for Shakespeare, wasn't she?" Kalina asked.

"She was a bright girl. She started reading before Patrick did and was on to novels by the time she'd hit second grade."

"How were they together? I mean I know having an older sister can be a challenge. I can't imagine having a sibling the same age as me, having to share everything."

Lois looked around the shop as if someone might overhear. "They could be civil if they wanted but I won't pretend things weren't tense between them. Paige was a bit domineering—"

"So she was a bully," Jimmy interrupted.

Lois shook her head. "Not to other children. It was strange if I'm being honest. She could be the sweetest thing you'd ever seen to other people and children her age. But when it was just her and Patrick, she could be quite nasty. I remember one time I found Patrick sitting at the bottom of the stairs with a bloody nose and a cut on his face. He said they'd been playing and Paige hit him. He begged me not to tell their parents."

"Did that happen often?" Kalina pressed.

"It seemed to come in waves. There would be weeks, months even, when they got on really well and then other times when he was coming to me with bumps and bruises."

Jimmy pulled out a notepad from his shirt pocket and jotted some notes down, alternating that with taking large gulps of his coffee. Lois twisted her cup between her hands.

"It sounds horrible but I have to say that when you called I had a feeling it was something like they'd survived. But a part of me hoped it had been Patrick. That boy didn't deserve the way his sister treated him."

"And you never confronted her about it?"

"Oh, I tried a few times but she acted all innocent and their parents wouldn't believe me."

Jimmy nodded and took another swig from his coffee. "What can you tell us about the day they went missing?'

"I told the police all about this back then."

"We know but we're hoping we can figure out how Paige might have survived."

Lois sighed and rubbed at her eyes. Kalina could tell she was losing her patience. "Everything was fine until the afternoon. They both said they wanted to go out on the beach and look for shells. It was one of the times they were getting along so I let them. The fresh air could do them good anyway. I had a lot of other things to take care of. I was the cleaning lady as well as the nanny and so I didn't notice until after it got dark that they hadn't come back inside.

"I went looking for them as soon as I realized they were gone. I couldn't find them anywhere. I didn't notice until the next day that the boat was missing. It didn't even occur to me that they knew how to start the thing, let alone maneuver it in open water. Besides, I don't think Patrick would have gotten on the boat unless Paige goaded him into it."

"Could they both swim?" Jimmy asked.

"Of course. They were like fish when they got in the ocean. Both very strong and skilled."

"So if the boat went off course or got pulled into a current, they'd be able to swim to shore," Kalina said.

"I'd think so." Tears glistened unshed in

her eyes. "Do you think maybe Patrick is alive, too?"

"It's possible. It would also shed some light on who might want her dead," Jimmy answered.

Lois gave a soft hiccup and the tears began to fall. Kalina reached across the table and took the woman's hand in comfort. Jimmy was on his feet retrieving napkins a moment later. Lois hiccupped again and sniffled a little more and then settled herself. Wiping at her eyes and cheeks, she said, "I'm so sorry. I just haven't thought about those poor children in a long time. The idea that both of them survived is just overwhelming."

"We understand. Ms. Hendrix, thank you for talking to us today. We should let you get back to your day," Jimmy said with a smile.

"Please find out who killed Paige."

"We'll do our best," Jimmy said and stood as she did.

Kalina reached out to stop her before she

got too far. "One last thing, do you know how Mr. and Mrs. Fischer died?"

Lois shook her head. "I'm afraid not. I believe Abigail had a sister ... Bethany Fairfax. She might know."

"Thank you."

Lois shuffled out of the coffee shop. Jimmy settled back into his chair as soon as she was gone and exhaled. "I think the brother might be alive, too."

"I got that feeling, too. I don't know what happened that got them Marblehead but something did. And if she was abusive towards him, it would give him a very clear motive for wanting her dead," Kalina agreed.

They stayed put until Jimmy finished his coffee. Kalina watched as people passed by the windows, oblivious to the world around them. A part of her missed the busy streets of Boston and the fast-paced lifestyle. But the part of her that returned to her roots and was content with her life as it was quickly shut down that longing. She had everything she'd always wanted back home in Ellesworth. Jimmy nudged her shoulder and brought her back to her surroundings.

"I just got a text from the captain. He wants me back at the station as soon as possible. He says he's got something interesting to share from the Maxwells."

Kalina heaved herself out of the chair and after a quick trip to the restroom she headed outside in the summer heat to wait for Jimmy to return with the car.

7

———————

Thanks to traffic headed out of the city to the beach, it took them longer than they'd hoped to get back to Ellesworth. It was almost noon by the time Jimmy pulled into the parking lot of the police station. Kalina made a beeline for the restroom while Jimmy headed into Chris's office. On her way back, she spotted a couple who were probably in their sixties sitting in the interview room. The door was open and no one seemed to be paying them any attention. She assumed they were the Maxwells. She heard Chris's voice in his office and she gravitated in that direction, eager to hear what had been interesting enough to make Jimmy race back to town.

"They got her a few months after the twins were presumed dead. She didn't speak for a while after that. Eventually, she told them her name was Verona," Chris said.

Kalina walked in and neither man reacted. She settled in one of the chairs across from her husband's desk and said, "I think she got the name Verona from Shakespeare. She was obsessed with his work according to Lois Hendrix."

"Interesting fact."

"Have you considered that maybe Patrick survived, too?" Jimmy asked.

Chris rubbed at his forehead. "I have but there's no evidence of that. At least not yet."

"Sir, did you bring us back here just to tell us she was mute for a while?" Jimmy asked.

"No. Mr. and Mrs. Maxwell shared with me that after she started talking again, they put her in therapy. They overheard her talking to herself, having whole conversations with herself, but when they asked her about it, it was like she didn't remember."

"Or she wouldn't admit to them that she was talking to herself. I know I'm not a doctor or anything but what if she didn't know Patrick survived? What if that was her way of coping with the loss of her brother?" Kalina said.

"It's as reasonable a theory as anything else," Chris agreed.

Before they could continue the conversation, the email inbox on Chris's computer flashed with a new message. The subject line, "Maxwell autopsy results," caught Kalina's attention and she leaned forward to try to get a better look as Chris opened the email. He skimmed the report too quickly for her to read anything, which annoyed her a little. Her annoyance level increased when he grabbed a tablet and strode out of the room without a word. She and Jimmy exchanged confused looks and trailed after him. Chris appeared on the monitor connected to the interview room where Mr. and Mrs. Maxwell sat side by side.

"We've just received some medical information on your daughter," Chris said and sat down opposite the couple. "She has old scars that are at least ten years old. Care to explain?"

Mrs. Maxwell pressed her fingers to her lips and glanced at her husband. She blinked rapidly several times before speaking. "We thought the therapy was working. She'd stopped talking to herself as much. But we didn't realize she'd started hurting herself. It was never enough to have her hospitalized for injuries but it was worrying."

"She got the treatment she needed and has been fine ever since," Mr. Maxwell insisted. "She was running a small beauty boutique. She was happy and successful."

Kalina bit her lip. They hadn't been able to share the knowledge that Paige had abused her brother. Chris would no doubt find it useful.

"Did Verona ever talk about a boy named Patrick to you?"

"No." Mr. Maxwell placed a hand on his wife's forearm. "Who is that?"

Chris set the tablet down and tapped the screen a couple of times. Through the monitor, Kalina watched as he presented them with a photo of Paige and Patrick from the local paper. "This is Verona and her twin brother, Patrick, shortly before they were presumed dead in a boating accident. Her name back then was Paige. Paige Fischer."

"Presumed dead?"

Chris nodded. "We only found out that Paige survived the boat accident when we ran your daughter's fingerprints."

"What about DNA? Have you done a DNA test?" Mrs. Maxwell's voice barely carried over the monitor's audio.

"We're still trying to find a DNA sample from when Paige went missing to compare," Chris answered.

"Do you think someone found out she was Paige and came after her?" Mr. Maxwell asked.

Chris was quiet for a moment, likely contemplating his next words before he answered. "We're working every angle. Did your daughter have any enemies that you were aware of?"

"No. Everyone liked her. After she got over her trauma, she was lovely to everyone. No one had a bad word to say about her." Mrs. Maxwell lapsed into quiet weeping.

"She was seeing someone new. She seemed quite serious about him," Mr. Maxwell added.

"Do you have his name?" Chris asked.

"No, I'm sorry."

Kalina looked away from the monitor to wipe at her eyes. Maybe it was the fact that she was about to become a mother, but she could feel Mrs. Maxwell's loss for her child. Jimmy pressed a tissue into her hand and smiled at him in thanks. She was vaguely aware of Chris telling the Maxwells that he would be in touch if he found anything else before they walked out, hand in hand. Neither of them gave Kalina or Jimmy a second glance as they moved past and to the front of the building.

"I need to call the techs and see if they've had any luck enhancing the surveillance footage," Chris said.

"I think you should take a break and get something to eat first. Come on, I'm buying," Kalina said. She wanted to fill him on what they'd learned from Lois Hendrix and maybe she could convince him to let her tag along when he interviewed Abigail Fischer's sister.

Chris opened his mouth, likely to protest, but Jimmy stepped up and gave them both a smile. "You get something to eat, Captain. I can hold down the fort here. Besides, I think Kal's got some really good information for you."

Kalina barely hid the smile on her face as she headed for the front of the building. She waited for Chris to join her, ready to enjoy a nice, leisurely stroll through town in the warm summer air. As she shielded her eyes from the sun, taking in the tree line that bordered the far edge of the station's parking lot, she could swear she saw someone watching her. That same sense that had settled over her in the cemetery hit her again. Was this Verona's killer? Had he still been in the cemetery when Kalina had been drawn to the site of Verona's murder? A shiver danced up her spine and she wrapped her arms around her torso to ward off the chill.

"You OK?" Chris asked as he finally joined her.

"Am I crazy or is there someone over there in the trees?" she asked in a whisper.

Chris followed her gaze but shook his head. "I don't see anyone. Come on, let's go find something to eat. I think maybe we're both just hungry."

8

———

A half hour later, they sat across from each other at home. They hadn't intended to go all the way home for food but somehow they'd just wandered by the restaurants that peppered both sides of Main Street.

"I need to tell you what we found out from Lois Hendrix," Kalina said as she blew the steam off the spoonful of soup in front of her.

"OK."

"She said that Paige was kind of a bully toward Patrick. It got to the point that it could have been considered abuse. But Patrick wouldn't let her tell their parents about it. Lois was convinced that Paige talked Patrick into getting on the boat that day."

"Did they know how to operate it?"

"Apparently."

Chris took a sip of his drink and studied the sandwich crumbs on his plate. "That might explain some of the behavior the Maxwells observed. The talking to herself. The self-harm. In fact, they said it sounded sometimes like she was arguing with someone."

"That's what I thought, too. She was used to bossing Patrick around and hurting him. Without him there, maybe she just started hurting herself."

"But eventually it stopped. The talking and the cutting."

"Maybe she just blocked that part of her life out and accepted that she wasn't Paige Fischer anymore. She embraced being Verona

Maxwell. I bet if you'd asked her anything about Paige, she wouldn't have a clue."

"You mean like multiple personalities?"

"Yeah. Something like that." She let out a sigh. "I bet it would be really helpful to see what she talked about with her psychologist."

"Those records would be difficult to get, especially with the patient dead."

"You have to try."

"I'll see what I can do."

"And you should talk to Abigail Fisher's sister, Bethany. Something about the way the Fischers died doesn't sit right with me. I tried to find their obituaries but there wasn't much there."

"It's worth looking into. Besides, maybe she kept something from Paige's childhood we could use for a DNA match. And I'm guessing you want to come along."

"If that's OK with you." She batted her lashes at him and smiled.

"As long as you aren't running off on your

own, I'll let you tag along. I need to keep an eye on you."

They lapsed into silence for a while and Kalina focused on her soup. The baby gave a kick or jab to her bladder once or twice but she was much calmer than she'd been earlier in the day. She had enjoyed most of being pregnant but she was eager to meet her daughter and to hold her tiny fingers in her own hand. That thought sparked an idea. "You have Patrick's fingerprints, right?"

"Yes. Why?"

"Have you thought about running his prints to see if they match any adults around the same age he'd be now? To at least rule him out as a suspect. I mean if there's nothing then there's probably a good chance he isn't the killer."

"I'll get someone on it." He pushed his chair back and disappeared from the kitchen.

In his absence, Kalina pulled out her phone and Googled Bethany Fairfax. Lucky for her, there was only one in the entire state of Massachusetts and she lived not too far away in Marblehead. That couldn't be a coincidence. She copied the address she'd found online to the Notes app on her phone and grabbed her purse. She nearly collided with Chris as she tried to leave the kitchen.

"I found Bethany Fairfax," she announced. His furrowed brow told her he didn't know who she was talking about. "Abigail Fischer's sister. Fairfax was her maiden name."

"Oh, right. I've got the lab running Patrick's prints. Where does Ms. Fairfax live?"

"Marblehead."

"Is that so?"

"Yep. Want to go see if the aunt has any idea what might have happened to the rest of her family?"

"I'll drive."

9

———

The trip out to Marblehead took about a half hour. The brief drive down the coast should have been pleasant, the weather had cooled off and a breeze blew through the open windows of the car, but Kalina couldn't shake the sense of dread squeezing her chest in a vice. All of the open water made her wonder what Patrick and Paige had endured on that fateful day twenty years ago. Had they been afraid of the open water? Had they lost control of the boat or were they out on the water with the intention of visiting their aunt?

"Kal, we're here." Chris's voice drew her back to the world.

"Did you call ahead?" she asked as he offered his hand to help her out of the car.

"No. I figured the element of surprise might be useful."

"Anything yet on the prints?"

"Nothing yet, no. The lab will call if and when they have something. But there is some good news. We have an angle on one of the surveillance cameras from the cemetery that got a good shot of the guy's face."

"That's great."

"So we've got that running, too."

They approached the single story, squat house that Google said belonged to Bethany Fairfax. Chris pulled out his badge and prepared to knock on the door. He didn't get the chance because a woman bustled out in a floral-print sundress and enormous sunhat.

"Oh, excuse me," she said.

"Are you Ms. Bethany Fairfax?" Chris asked.

"I am. Who are you?"

"My name is Captain Christian Harper. I'm with the Ellesworth police department. I was hoping I could speak with you for a few minutes about your niece and nephew."

Bethany took a step back into her front hall. "My niece and nephew died twenty years ago."

"I'm afraid that's not true. Your niece, Paige, was recently murdered. Please, it's just a few questions."

Bethany didn't look willing to give in until Kalina made a show of pressing a hand to her belly and grimacing. The older woman gave a sympathetic look and waved them inside.

"Thank you," Chris whispered just loud enough for Kalina to hear.

"Bet you're glad you brought me along," Kalina replied.

Bethany led them to a small living room cluttered with second-hand furniture and Tiffany lamps. It wasn't the set up Kalina had expected for a woman from a wealthy family. She eased herself onto the loveseat positioned beneath the mantle and Chris settled in a recliner next to her. Bethany paced back and forth in front of them for a few minutes before finally sitting on a wooden stool, setting her hat on the low coffee table between them.

"Thank you," Kalina said, indicating the seat.

"Sure. When are you due?"

"A few weeks." She looked around the room as best she could and caught a photo of Bethany and a young man who looked vaguely familiar. "Do you have children?"

"A son. Logan. He's grown up now and moved out."

"Ms. Fairfax, I know this news must be a shock for you but I really need your help," Chris interrupted.

Bethany smoothed out the hem of her dress and twisted her fingers into the fabric. "I'm not sure how much help I'll be, but OK."

"What do you know about what happened to your niece and nephew?"

"They went out on the family boat and never came home."

"Do you happen to have anything that belonged to Paige as a child? A lock of hair or a toothbrush for when she stayed over?"

"Why? I thought you said she was dead."

"The fingerprints match but we want to be absolutely sure."

"I don't. I'm sorry. They never really stayed over here. Abigail, my sister, didn't like them being away from home."

That seemed odd to Kalina, given how much the Fischers seemed to travel and leave their children in Lois Hendrix's care. But she said nothing. She caught Bethany's gaze flit to a photo of Logan as a teenager. He was sandy-haired and suntanned with a broad grin. Still, she couldn't shake the familiar feeling. Much like she'd had when he found Paige in the cemetery. "How'd your son react to the news that his cousins had died? They look like they'd be about the same age," Kalina said.

"He was upset of course. We all were. It was such a shock."

"But Paige didn't die. She was taken into foster care and adopted. She ran a successful beauty shop until someone killed her," Chris said.

"I don't know what I can tell you. Until you showed up at my door, I had no idea she was even alive."

"This may seem like a strange question but do you know how your sister and brother-in-law died?"

"I think it was a faulty carbon monoxide detector in the house. That's what the police said when they came to notify me."

"When was that?"

"I don't remember. A year ago maybe."

"Did Logan get along with Paige?" Chris asked.

"Yes. Why are you asking about Logan? I thought this was about Paige."

"Ma'am, is it possible that your nephew could have survived too?"

"I don't know. I think I want you to leave. I'm sorry I can't be more help."

Kalina opened her mouth to press the issue but Chris shook his head and offered his hand to help her up. They started for the front of the house when Kalina stopped. "Could I use your bathroom?"

"Last door on the left down that hallway."

Kalina took off down the hall at a brisk waddle. She really did need to use the bathroom but she figured she could also use the time to look around. The hallway was lined with more photos of Logan as a teenager. There was even one of him graduating from college. Oddly, there were no photos of him younger than eleven or twelve. The suspicious part of her mind tried to convince her that Logan was actually Patrick but it couldn't rationalize why Bethany would have kept his survival a secret. Surely she would have returned him to his parents. She passed a room on the right with a partially closed door. She nudged it open with her foot and took in the room of a guy in his late twenties. The walls were bare except for a single photo of Logan and Bethany. There was a laptop sitting open on the desk. When she hit the Enter key to wake the machine up, it prompted her for a password.

"Damn."

The desk had a center drawer that she eased open to find a print-out from a dating website. The figure in the profile picture was unmistakably Verona Maxwell. The baby chose that moment to press more insistently on her bladder and she had to retreat across the hall to the bathroom. She returned to the living room to find Chris, keys already in hand, and Bethany with her hat back on her head.

They left through the front door and said nothing until they were back in the car. Kalina watched as Bethany strode up the street at a brisk pace.

"Well that was a bust," Chris muttered.

"Not entirely. I looked around a little bit while I was heading to the bathroom. There aren't any pictures of Logan before the age of ten. And it looks like Bethany lied to us about Logan moving out. There's a room that looks lived in. I saw a computer but it was locked. There's definitely something off about all of this."

"You think Logan is Patrick."

"I got that same feeling looking at pictures of him that I did with Paige. And she was definitely avoiding talking about Logan as a young child. There has to be a reason."

"It's looking more like we have a suspect. We just have to find him."

"I know it's not definitive but what if you used aging software on a picture of Patrick at ten and see if it looks like Logan now. And compare it to the surveillance photo."

Chris leaned over and kissed her cheek. "I knew I married you for a reason."

"There's something else. I found a printout of a profile for Verona on a dating website in the top desk drawer. Even if Logan isn't Patrick, he still found Verona and it's worth talking to him."

Chris put the car into drive and did a quick U-turn so they could head out of town. "So let's see if we can find Logan Fairfax."

10

Kalina expected Chris to be on the phone to the precinct giving orders but the hands free set remained unused. They spent the first ten minutes travelling in silence before Chris turned to look at her..

"How are you feeling?"

"I'm fine, Chris. I was only pretending earlier to get Bethany to talk to us."

"All of this exertion just stresses me out. I don't want anything to happen to you."

"I'm fine. We've got a few weeks to go anyway."

Just as Chris pulled onto the highway, his phone buzzed with an incoming call from the precinct. Kalina reached over and tapped the phone and set it to speaker.

"Hey Captain, is this a good time?" Jimmy's voice filled the car through the speaker system.

"Yeah, it's fine, Jimmy. What's up?"

"I ran those prints like you asked and it came back with a match."

Kalina and Chris shared an expectant glance before he said, "Go on."

"The prints matched a guy with a criminal record named Logan Fairfax."

Kalina bit down hard on her lip to keep from exclaiming that she'd been right. Chris nodded at her as he switched lanes.

"What's the record for?"

"Misdemeanor possession. We've got an address in Marblehead."

"His mother's address. We were just there."

"Sir? I thought you were going to interview their aunt."

"I'll explain when we get back. See if you can find any other address on Fairfax. We'll be at the station in about fifteen minutes." He jabbed the screen to end the call.

"Shouldn't we go back and try to get more out of Bethany?" Kalina asked.

"Not yet. We need to see if we can get a location on Logan first."

"She could have tipped him off."

"At this point she only knows that her niece survived the accident too and someone's killed her."

"But wouldn't you think she'd put two and two together?"

"If we go back now, she'll shut down more."

Kalina ran a hand through her hair and stared out the passenger side window, trying to sort through the thoughts racing around her brain. How could Bethany not know the truth? And why hadn't she taken Patrick back to his parents when he showed up?

"Did you notice what dating website Verona had an account with?" Chris's voice interrupted her thoughts.

"It might have been OK Cupid. I didn't notice to be honest."

"That's all right. We'll get Verona's laptop and see who she was talking to."

"I can't imagine being separated for all those years and then they find each other on a dating website. Do you think they were actually attracted to each other?"

Chris shrugged his right shoulder. "Maybe. But if Logan knew she was Paige, he was probably using it to stalk her."

"I wonder if she realized who he was before she died."

"Something tells me he wouldn't let her go before she knew."

The conversation died down again as they got off the highway and pulled onto Main Street. "Can you drop me at the shop? I want to check in on things and I think I need to rest for a while," she said before he could make the turn toward the police station.

"Of course."

She pulled out her phone and sent a quick text to Jillian, letting her know she was on the way. There was no response before they pulled up in front of the shop's front door.

"Make sure you put your feet up and drink plenty of water," Chris called as she closed the passenger side door.

The bell above the front door 'dinged' as she entered and Jillian looked up from her phone.

"Just got your text. Shouldn't you be at home?"

"Why? I'd just be sitting around going crazy when I could be here obsessing over work."

"Or Paige Fischer?" Jillian slid the tablet they used for transactions across the counter.

Kalina picked it up and took it into the game room so she could put her feet up. Jillian followed after her, not saying a word. The tablet's screen displayed a news article from the town's online edition, published only a few hours ago.

Lost Twin Found ... Murdered

By: Heather Casey, Staff Reporter

In the late morning hours of June 10th, a twenty-year-old mystery unraveled. As many in town will remember, ten-year-old Paige Fischer and her brother perished at sea twenty years ago. But a woman with Paige's fingerprints was discovered in the cemetery by someone close to the local authorities.

"Damn, how did they find out?" Kalina groaned.

"People in town talk. I'm assuming once people found out this Verona woman was found at the Fischer family grave site, speculation began running wild," Jillian answered.

Kalina kept reading.

The details are still unclear as to how Paige survived the boat accident that claimed her brother's life or who would want her dead all these years later. Some in town speculate that Paige returned home to mourn her parents who passed away last year under suspicious circumstances. Others question if Patrick may have survived as well. And if that is true, why would they not have come home sooner?

A local school teacher recalled the twins as being quiet and reserved although there was always something about Paige that set the teacher on edge. "I remember she had this quiet intensity about her for such a young child. Like there was something deep down she was hiding." And of Patrick, the teacher noted, "He always looked scared to me. Afraid of his own shadow, especially when his sister was around. I should have done something back then. I knew something didn't seem right." Was it this inner secret that led to her death now? Could it be her brother came back for some twisted sort of revenge?

This story is developing. Please check back for updates.

"Chris is going to have a field day with this reporter. I can't imagine who talked to her. The guys on the force know better."

"What about you?" Jillian raised a brow at her sister.

"Me? I've been with Jimmy or Chris the whole day. And I am not going to talk to the press. Paige may have been a bully to her brother ... abusive even"—she tossed the tablet on a nearby table—"but she doesn't need to be dragged through the mud like this. No one, no matter how terrible, deserves to be murdered."

"Kal, I don't think that's what they were saying," Jillian said, her tone placating.

"I know you're right but it just makes me so angry. The way they just threw around all of these accusations like they're fact."

"But from what you said, it sounds like it isn't just speculation."

Kalina rubbed at the pressure building in her temples. She didn't want to argue with her sister over this. "Just forget it, OK?"

Jillian held up her hands in surrender. "Fine. I think all of this detective work is stressing you out. It's not good for you."

"These were kids we knew, Jill. Don't we owe it to them to find out what happened?"

"Yes. I guess they deserve to have their story told, even if it isn't a happy ending."

Jillian disappeared back to the front of the store just as Kalina's phone buzzed, displaying Chris's work number. She answered on the second ring. "Hi. Before you ask, yes, I've got my feet up." Breath caught in her throat as a sharp pain lanced across her belly. She grimaced and bit down on her lip to keep from groaning audibly through the pain.

"Good. I figured you'd like to know we got a hit on Verona's computer. We found a bunch of messages on OK Cupid between her and Logan. It doesn't seem like she knew who he was based on the messages but they were definitely in contact."

The pain subsided and she blew out a breath. "Have you had any luck tracking him down?"

"We're working on it. The last communication between them was from a day before the murder. They agreed to meet in town.'

"Did they say why here? Neither of them was living in town anymore."

"It sounded like Logan wanted to check out the beach. Or so he says." Muffled voices crackled over the phone connection. "I think we may have found something on his location."

"Keep me posted."

11

———————

Half an hour later, restless energy and a sense of anticipation compelled Kalina out of the shop and on a walk along Main Street. The pain had come and gone a time or two but she was doing her best to ignore it. She assumed Chris had found Logan by now. She was curious to know how it had happened. Had he known he'd found his sister when he and Verona first connected? And if he hadn't, when did it click for him?

She strolled along the street with the fading sunlight falling in little patterns on the sidewalk for a while longer until she found herself standing at the front lawn of the Fischer estate. For a place that had been vacant for over a year, it looked oddly lived in. The front mat was askew and the curtains in the front room had been opened to allow the natural light in. She didn't get the feeling that Bethany Fairfax had been by to keep up appearances. Keeping Patrick a secret sent the very clear message that she didn't approve of her sister and her brother-in-law and their parenting style. Before she could even set foot on the front walk, wailing sirens erupted nearby and a squad car came screaming up the street. Jimmy jumped out of the passenger side before the car had come to a full stop. Chris followed suit moments later and Kalina stepped out of their way. From somewhere at the back of the house, a door slammed loud enough to echo throughout the yard.

"He's going around back," Chris called and Jimmy took off like a shot.

Chris moved methodically toward the front of the house and tried the front door. It swung inward on oiled hinges, barely betraying his entrance. His shout of "Police Department!" ruined any chance of stealth he had.

Kalina watched her husband disappear into the house and her heart beat faster in her chest. Until he came out, gun holstered, she couldn't breathe. Jimmy appeared moments later dragging along a man in his late 20s who looked like Logan Fairfax with his hands cuffed behind his back.

"I didn't do anything!" Logan shouted.

Jimmy said nothing as he pushed him into the backseat of the cruiser. Chris stopped on his way to the car to place a hand on Kalina's arm. "What are you doing here?'

"I don't know. I was just out for a walk and

ended up—" Breath caught in her chest as pain shot through her belly. She bent double until it passed.

"What's wrong?"

"Nothing, I'm fine. It's just a little pain."

"You don't look fine. Has this happened before?"

Kalina met Chris's gaze and knew she couldn't lie to him about this. "A few times. Maybe four times in the last hour. But, really, it passes and I'm OK."

"Honey, it sounds like you've started to have contractions. We need to get you to the hospital."

"No. It's too early. And my water hasn't broken."

Chris turned and waved at Jimmy. "Call for another car and get him back to the station."

"OK but why, sir?"

"We're going to the hospital."

Jimmy's face broke out in a broad grin and he pulled Logan from the backseat of the cruiser with one hand, the other already reaching for his radio. Kalina didn't protest as Chris ushered her into the passenger seat and they took off at what most would consider an unsafe speed. With the flip of a switch, the sirens blared to life, announcing their presence.

"The siren isn't necessary, Chris," Kalina said but Chris's attention was focused on the trip across town to the hospital.

He pulled the car to a screeching halt in front of the Emergency entrance. The siren still wailed and a nurse came running with a wheelchair. Taking a slow breath, Kalina un-buckled the seatbelt and calmly exited the car.

"I can walk, thank you," she said and stalked past the nurse.

Ten minutes later, they were escorted to a private room and Kalina settled on the bed to wait for the doctor to check in. Chris paced anxiously by the window.

"Sit down," she said and patted the bed next to her.

"Sorry. I'm just nervous," he said and settled next to her, wrapping his arm around her shoulders. "I don't think either of us expected this to happen quite so soon."

"I think Jill was right and this case is stressing me out," Kalina said and rubbed her belly.

Chris nodded but stayed silent. The way his gaze still drifted to the window told her he wasn't just anxious about the baby. He didn't like not being involved in the rest of the investigation.

"You're worried about how the interrogation is going, aren't you?"

"Jimmy's grown up a lot in the last year. He's capable of handling it."

"I know that. And I'm glad you see that too. Sometimes he doesn't think you've paid attention to his progress. But even though you know he's capable you don't like to let cases go."

"I guess we've both got a little control freak in us."

Kalina snorted. "A little?"

He laughed and the little lines around his eyes crinkled. "OK, so a lot. But I have to realize that investigating the cases isn't really my job anymore. I'm not a detective. I need to let them do the work."

"Letting go of what you love is hard." A lesson she was learning the hard way. Helping to solve these cases wasn't a calling in the same way that Chris was called to police work, but it satisfied a passion in her. But as she'd told Mrs. Grant, she had no choice but to give it up ... at least for now.

A quick knock on the door brought the conversation to a halt. Kalina's obstetrician appeared in the doorway, an ultrasound machine just in view. "How are we feeling?"

"OK right now."

"Any more pain since you came in?"

"No."

"Well, we're going to check you out anyway and figure out what's going on. I'm going to have you get undressed and we'll take a look."

Kalina stripped down, wrapping the hospital robe around her body before settling back on the bed. Chris stood by her side, his hand wrapped around hers. He squeezed it tight as the doctor strapped on a fetal heart monitor and began a physical exam.

"Well, you look to be a couple centimeters dilated but we're nowhere near delivering this baby."

"Is the baby all right?" Kalina asked.

The doctor pointed to the steady heartbeat on the monitor. "Everything looks good with the heartbeat. There's no sign of fetal distress."

Kalina breathed a sigh of relief. She didn't

even react to the cool gel that the ultrasound technician squirted on her bare abdomen. "Everything looks fine. I'm going to keep you here another couple of hours just to be sure but my guess is you had Braxton Hicks contractions."

"So it was a false alarm," Chris said.

The doctor nodded. "Most likely. But like I said, we'll keep her here for a few hours just to be sure."

"Thank you," Kalina said.

Chris sagged against the bed as soon as they were alone. "Thank God."

"Honey, they're going to let me leave in a couple hours. I can have my mom come by and give me a ride home. Go back to the station."

"No, I should be here with you."

Somewhere down the hall an alarm blared. Simultaneously, Chris's phone began to ring. He checked the display and stepped closer to the window for better reception. "Hello, this is Captain Harper."

Kalina strained to hear what was being said on the other end of the call but he had the volume turned down low and he was facing away from her, distorting her view of his facial expressions in the window. "No I'll meet you there. Text me when you've got a room number."

"What's going on?" she asked over the continued blare of the alarm.

"That was the officer on desk duty at the station. Jimmy had to call the paramedic to come sedate Logan."

"What? Why?"

"Apparently, when Jimmy started questioning him about Patrick Fischer, he lost it and attacked Jimmy."

"Oh God, is Jimmy OK?"

"I'm not sure. The officer said he had some lacerations. I told them to text me when they have more information."

"Did they bring Logan here?"

"Yeah, he's being admitted into the psych ward. Maybe with a doctor's help we can sort out what really happened and what prompted him to kill his sister after all these years."

Fifteen minutes later, Chris had headed off in search of Jimmy. Kalina remained in hospital. The pain had returned and was coming in closer bouts. Her doctor had been nonplussed about the sudden change. At least she was allowed to walk around. In fact, her doctor had insisted that moving around would help things progress. So after sending a text to Chris, she wandered the halls until she found Jimmy sitting in a curtained off area in the very back of the Emergency Department with a couple of gauze bandages on his arm.

"How are you doing?" he asked when he spotted Kalina.

"OK. Apparently it wasn't as much of a false alarm as we thought. The doctor said walking is supposed to help labor progress." She pointed to his arm. "How about you? What happened?"

"It looks worse than it is. He got a hold of my keys. I shouldn't have kept a pocket knife on there." Jimmy looked at Chris but didn't meet his gaze. "He jabbed me a couple times as I was trying to calm him down. Started yelling about how I wasn't going to hurt Patrick. I think he's nuts."

"We'll let the professionals decide that," Chris said and clapped Jimmy on the shoulder. "You should take the rest of the day off. We'll talk about this when the case is wrapped up."

Kalina saw the hint of fear on Jimmy's face when Chris turned away and flagged down a nurse.

"Everything will be fine," she whispered and gave the hand of his injured arm a light squeeze that quickly turned into a vice grip as a contraction came on.

"Uh, boss, something's happening."

In a flash, Chris was at her side, rubbing her back as she breathed through the pain. It passed and she relinquished her grip on Jimmy's hand. He massaged the angry, red marks she'd left on his palm.

"Sorry about that," she said.

"Let's get you back to the maternity ward," Chris said and nudged her forward.

"Is it really not as bad as it looks?" she asked as they walked side by side through the pristine hospital halls.

"Yeah, it's minor."

"Has there been anything new on Logan? Has anyone talked to him?"

"The last I heard they were evaluating him. But you don't need to worry about that right now. I promise, Paige will get justice. Right now you need to focus on bringing our baby girl into this world, OK?"

"OK."

"Don't be too hard on Jimmy when you talk to him. He's a good officer and he just made a mistake."

"I'm not mad at him. He already knows what he should have done differently and I don't have any doubt that he will learn from the mistake. Just between you and me, I was planning on giving him his detective's shield in a few months."

"That's fast."

"He does good work. And I think the promotion will help propel his career forward. Sometimes you need someone to take a chance on you to show you just what you're capable of. And he kind of reminds me of myself when I was an officer. He's got that same drive."

"I'm glad." They arrived back at her room to find Jillian and AJ sitting by the window. "You guys didn't have to come."

"Mom insisted you not be alone. And I figured you could use your big sister here," Jillian answered and rushed over to give Kalina a tight embrace.

Her sister's mood had obviously improved since their squabble over the newspaper article. AJ stayed put and quiet, gazed focused on his phone, as Jillian let go and gave Chris a hug too.

"You doing all right, kiddo?" Kalina asked.

"Huh? I was just reading this article about the woman who was killed," he said and offered his phone.

A pang of dread tightened Kalina's chest as she looked at the screen but it disappeared immediately. It was the same article that had gotten her worked up before. Unfortunately, there were no edits or retractions noted. Whoever was handling the PR for the police hadn't succeeded in getting the article removed. Her nephew kept glancing between the medical equipment and her stomach.

"Why don't you go see if there's a cafeteria or something and get your mom and Chris some coffee or something?" Kalina suggested.

Relief washed over his face and he darted out of the room. Jillian sat on the edge of the bed and motioned for Kalina to get under the covers.

"How far apart are your contractions?"

"About ten minutes. They're more irritating than anything."

"If you're anything like me, they'll speed up before you know it. I thought it was never going to end with AJ."

"Let's hope you're right."

Chris's phone beeped with a new text

message. "The attendant in the psych ward needs to talk to me about the case."

"Go. I'll be here when you get back."

"Call me if anything ... big happens," he said.

She nodded and he took off at a sprint. Jillian busied herself with plumping Kalina's pillows and making sure the bed was at a comfortable angle.

"I was a little worried about you earlier. You just took off," Jillian said.

"I'm sorry. I needed the air."

"Where did you go?"

"It's going to sound crazy but I ended up at the Fischer house. Logan ... Patrick ... whatever he's going by was staying there. I didn't mean to go there but I guess my subconscious had other ideas."

"They found him though?"

"They did. He got violent when Jimmy tried to question him."

"I wonder what happened to him that made him snap like that."

"I don't know. Maybe he'd blocked out all the trauma and then seeing her again after all these years triggered those memories. I'm sure Chris will figure out what happened when he talks to the doctor."

"I still can't believe they both survived that boat accident. I'd really like to know how that happened."

"If the doctors can get him to talk I'm sure we'll find out." Kalina grit her teeth as another contraction hit her.

"Do you want me to call a nurse to see about getting an epidural?"

"Not yet. They said they'd do it the next time they checked me."

On cue, a nurse stuck her head through the door. "How're we doing in here?"

"I think I'd like that epidural now," Kalina answered.

"Let me grab the doctor and we'll take a peek."

By the time the doctor had checked her and the anesthesiologist had administered the drugs, her contractions were only four minutes apart. Chris was nowhere to be seen despite several texts from Kalina and Jillian. AJ hung back just outside the doorway, watching.

"You can come in, honey," Jillian said.

"No, that's OK. I'd just be in the way."

Kalina was aware of another contraction passing through her as she studied her nephew's face. "Kiddo, I need you to do me a huge favor and go find your uncle for me. The baby is going to be here soon and if he's not with me to witness it, we're going to have another homicide on our hands."

AJ's face brightened. "You got it!"

"Thanks," Jillian whispered as her son took off.

"Like I said before, teenage boys and birth don't usually mix."

Ten minutes later, AJ marched into the room with a triumphant grin on his face. "Got him!"

"Sorry! I'm here." Chris rushed to her side and grabbed her left hand.

"We texted you. What's going on?"

"I thought we were making progress with Logan but he's shut down again. I didn't hear my phone go off. It was on silent."

Kalina gave him an annoyed sidelong glare as another contraction—this much closer together—faintly rippled through her belly. He'd been the one to tell them to call if anything big had changed. She bit her lower lip to keep from snapping at him. It wouldn't do anything but frustrate him.

Her doctor reappeared with a new nurse, both in scrubs and face masks. "I'm just going to check to see how far you've progressed. It might be time to start pushing."

"OK."

Kalina blew out a slow breath as the

doctor examined her. Chris's grip was steady and present, making some of her irritation dissipate. He was here for the important part.

"Everything looks ready, so I'm going to need you to start pushing when you feel the urge, Kalina."

She had no idea how she was supposed to know but apparently the rest of her body was in tune with what was happening because a few minutes later her knees were raised and her chin was pressed to her chest.

"Nine. Ten. And relax," her doctor instructed.

Kalina lay back against the pillow, beads of sweat moistening her upper lip. "How much longer?"

"You're doing great." Chris brushed a strand of sweaty hair out of her face.

"Push again."

Kalina bore down and this time she could feel something change and move. She was so focused on the push she didn't register the sounds of encouragement around her.

"One more big push like that and I think we're going to have our baby," her doctor prompted.

She pushed one last time. The haze of the experience fell away as a wail filled the room.

"Our baby girl cried," Chris said.

Kalina turned to look at him and saw tears streaming down his cheeks. Her husband clearly didn't care that he was sobbing. He made no attempt to wipe them away. Instead, he released his grip on her hand and accepted the tiny, squirming baby wrapped in a hospital blanket. He settled their little girl on Kalina's chest.

"Welcome to the world, little lady," Chris whispered and stroked the baby's cheek.

"What are you going to call her?" Kalina jumped a little at the sound of her sister's voice.

"Nina Elise."

"That's a beautiful name."

Chris's attention diverted from the baby for a split second as his phone buzzed. "I'll get it later," he said.

"Take it. You're still working the case."

"He's not going anywhere."

"Chris, please just answer it."

He bent and kissed Nina's head before stepping out into the hallway. With his back to her, Kalina couldn't see his face. But his shoulders tensed and his back went rigid. Whatever was being communicated wasn't making him happy. The nurse took Nina from Kalina's arms.

"Where are you taking her?" Kalina's tone came out more desperate than she'd intended.

"To the nursery. Your husband is welcome to come with me."

"He's busy. AJ and I will go and keep an eye on her," Jillian offered.

The panic that had begun to tighten Kalina's chest subsided. At least someone would be watching over her daughter. Chris ended his call just as the nurse, Jillian and AJ walked by.

"What's wrong?" Kalina asked when she saw his face.

"Bethany Fairfax is here demanding to see her son."

"What are you going to do?"

He pinched the bridge of his nose and exhaled. "I don't know."

"Maybe you should talk to her."

"I don't know what good it will do. I mean I'm fairly certain she didn't have anything to do with Paige's death."

"But she kept Patrick from his parents. Even if he wanted to stay that's got to be illegal."

"It will be a hard charge to prove. And the Fischers are dead now. They aren't going to agree to file anything."

"But you have to do something."

He held up his hands. "I get it, Kal. Calm

down. I'll talk to her and see what happens. You rest."

"I don't want to rest. I want to know what happened."

"I'll make you a deal. I'll talk to Bethany and let you know what happens if you promise to stay here and rest for a while. You just had a baby."

"Fine."

13

Kalina fell into a light doze as soon as Chris left. She only awoke when she felt a hand on her arm. Blinking the sleep from her eyes, she saw Jimmy standing over her.

"What is it?" Her tongue felt thick.

"Ms. Fairfax wants to speak with you."

Kalian dragged herself into a sitting position as Bethany Fairfax entered the room looking solemn. Her eyes were rimmed red from crying.

"Congratulations," Bethany said.

"Thanks. What did you want to talk to me about?"

Bethany pulled a chair over to the edge of the bed and sat down. Her shoulders sagged and her mouth turned down at the edges. "I've spoken with Captain Harper. I realize now what I did was wrong and I'm going to take responsibility for it. I just wanted a child of my own so badly and when Patrick turned up on my doorstep, I took it as a sign. I loved him like my own but I see now he was broken."

"You knew how Paige treated him then?"

"He'd wake up from nightmares about her."

"Why didn't his parents do anything about it? I know Lois Hendrix kept the secret but surely they had to realize something was off."

"After they became parents they realized neither of them were very good at it. So they just got a nanny and said that was that. They played the grieving parents well enough but I don't doubt for a moment they were relieved when they were gone."

"I still don't understand why you needed to tell me all of this."

"Logan needs to admit to what he's done but he won't talk to the police and I made a decision a long time to ago not to force him to be Patrick anymore. But he liked you. Maybe you could reach him."

Kalina looked to Jimmy. "The captain's already approved it. He'll be there with you."

"I'll try."

Ten minutes later—after a quick wash in the bathroom and some fresh clothes—Kalina sat in another hospital room staring at Logan Fairfax handcuffed to a bedrail. He was still in the clothes he'd been wearing when Jimmy arrested him. He wouldn't meet her gaze and his face was set in a stony mask. So unlike the little boy she remembered.

"Logan, my name is Kalina. I knew you

when you were younger. Do you remember me?"

"I've got no idea who you are, lady."

"No, I guess you wouldn't. But Patrick would, isn't that right?"

His face twitched, as if he wanted to acknowledge who she was but a part of him wouldn't let him. She supposed that was the truth; that he'd developed another personality to protect himself from his sister's abuse, even the memories.

"Patrick, I know you can hear me and I know you were a good kid. You just had a lot of bad things happen to you."

He turned and his face had relaxed. The ghost of a smile was on his lips and his eyes shone with unshed tears. "I remember you now. You read to me that summer." His voice had gone up several octaves. The little boy really had never grown up.

"Yes. I did." She reached out to take his

hand gently in her own. "Do you mind if I just talk to you for a little while?"

"OK."

"I know it's scary to talk about but can you tell me what happened on the boat? A lot of people were really worried about you."

He chewed his lower lip. The inner war began again but, based on his expression, Patrick was still in the driver seat. "Paige wanted to go out on the boat. I told her it was a bad idea without Mom and Dad or Lois. But she didn't care. She wanted to go and she made me come too. She pinched me really hard"—he touched his upper arm—"until I said I'd go."

"I'm sorry she hurt you. Do you remember what happened once you were on the boat?"

"We took it out into the water but the current was too strong and it pushed us away from the beach. We got all turned around and then she started laughing. She thought it was a game. She dared me to jump off the side of the boat. I told her I wouldn't and then she pushed me. The next thing I know I'm on a beach."

"And that's when your Aunt Bethany found you?"

"Yeah."

"Thank you so much for telling me that." Kalina released her grip, anticipating a change in his demeanor when she asked her next question. "Do you remember meeting Paige again recently?"

Logan, the stony-faced protector, returned. "I knew it was her the moment I met her."

"Did you reach out to her on the dating site?"

"No, she found me. I let her think she was winning me over. Like we had a connection. Hell, I even let her kiss me on the first date. Had to drink a lot to get that image out of my head."

"What made you decide to kill her?" She caught Chris out of the corner of her eye, watching the progress. Bethany had been right. She was able to get him to open up.

"She laughed and grabbed my arm. Stupid bitch. I knew then she hadn't changed. She could put on nice clothes and call herself Verona but she would always still be Paige. I couldn't let her hurt him again. And so I convinced her to go on a trip to the beach. I didn't tell her where until we got there. She thought it was a joke until I showed her our graves. Right next to our parents. I made her admit she knew who I was right before I killed her."

"They died last year."

Logan grinned. "They never saw it coming. I had to work up to that one though, find the right way of doing it so they wouldn't know who it was. After all, they never really saw him growing up."

Chris stepped into the room and motioned for Kalina to leave. "You did great. Thank you."

She expected Logan to protest as she left

when Chris began reading him his rights but he looked resigned to his fate. Much like Bethany had. They'd been carrying the weight of the family's tragedies for too long and now it was being lifted. Kalina wound her way through the hospital to the nursery and found Jillian and AJ standing watch over Nina's bassinet through the window.

Jillian looked over and smiled. "What happened?"

"We solved the case. Paige lured Patrick out on the boat that day and pushed him overboard. He spent the last year planning his revenge on his parents and sister."

"That's messed up," AJ said.

"It is, but at least now we know the truth. And now Chris and I can focus on being parents." She waved to her daughter through the glass. "But I think we've solved our last case."

When Reverend Margot Quade returns to her small town, she lands right at the center of a murder. Can she help solve the case? Grab Into the Lion's Den and start unraveling the mystery today!

GET FREE CONTENT

Sign up for my newsletter by clicking here to be kept up-to-date with my latest releases and receive your copy of Toil and Trouble as a free gift.

All Hallow's Eve brings dangerous secrets. Can Kalina get to the bottom of the mystery?

Subscribe and find out now!

A GEEKS AND THINGS COZY MYSTERY
Toil and Trouble
S.E. BIGLOW

ABOUT THE AUTHOR

S.E. Biglow is the pen name of *USA Today* bestselling author Sarah Biglow. She lives in Massachusetts with her husband and son. She is a licensed attorney and spends her days combatting employment discrimination as an

Investigator with the Massachusetts Commission Against Discrimination.

You can find an up-to-date list of all my books here

9 781955 988087